I AM READ

The Ugly Egg

LOU KUENZLER

ILLUSTRATED BY

DAVID HITCH

KINGFISHER
NEW YORK

To Lily and Isabel—always hatching
your own stories—love, Mum—L. K.
In memory of Rose—D. H.

KINGFISHER
LONDON & NEW YORK

Text copyright © 2009 by Lou Kuenzler
Illustrations copyright © 2009 by David Hitch
Published in the United States by Kingfisher,
175 Fifth Ave., New York, NY 10010
Kingfisher is an imprint of Macmillan Children's Books, London.

Distributed in the U.S. by Macmillan, 175 Fifth Ave., New York, NY 10010
Distributed in Canada by H.B. Fenn and Company Ltd., 34 Nixon Road, Bolton, Ontario L7E 1W2

Library of Congress Cataloging-in-Publication data has been applied for.

ISBN: 978-0-7534-6284-3

Kingfisher books are available for special promotions and premiums. For details contact:
Special Markets Department, Macmillan, 175 Fifth Avenue, New York, NY 10010.

For more information, please visit www.kingfisherpublications.com

First American Edition November 2009
Printed in China
10 9 8 7 6 5 4 3 2 1

Contents

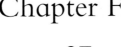

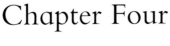

Chapter One

WHOOSH! The Arctic wind blew,
straight from the North Pole.
Posy the little puffin shivered.
"Brrrrrrrrr! I'm cold!" she said.
"Stay in your nest," warned the

Snow Goose from her rock, high up above. "Keep your eggs warm!"

"I don't have any eggs," said Posy.

"No eggs?" said the Snow Goose. "But this is a nest site. *Everyone* here has eggs!"

5

Posy looked around. The Snow Goose was right. All the other birds were sitting in nests. All the other birds had eggs to keep warm.

"I tried to lay an egg," said Posy. "But I couldn't."

"Nonsense!" said the Snow Goose. "Laying an egg is easy. Watch me!"

"Follow her *egg*sample!" black-and-white Mrs. Loon said with a laugh.

The Snow Goose wiggled her tail.

POP!

Out came a snow white egg.

"See! It's simple!" The Snow Goose peered down at Posy. "I've laid six eggs already," she boasted. This new one makes . . . seven! A fine brood." Posy wished the Snow Goose would stop showing off.

"I'd be happy with one egg," Posy said to herself. "Just one egg of my own!"

Chapter Two

"Walk in a circle," said the bossy Snow Goose. "That will help you lay an egg." "All right," said Posy. "I'll give it a try."

Around and around went Posy. But no egg came.

"Bob up and down!" said Mrs. Loon.

"That's what I always do."

Posy bobbed up and down.

"Again!" said the Snow Goose.

"Again!"

Up and down
went Posy.
But no egg came.

"Wiggle your behind!" Mrs. Loon said, giggling. "Wiggle it from side to side!"

Cha, cha, cha!

Posy wiggled her behind.

She wiggled it around and around.

Cha Cha Cha

But still no egg came.

"Don't give up!" said Mrs. Loon.
"You've almost got it! You'll see!"
Posy shook her head."It's no use," she
said. "I just can't lay an egg."
Posy tucked her head under her wing.
She didn't want the others to see her cry.

After a while, she looked up. A shape
caught her eye . . . something big and
oval, out on the ice.

"What's that?" she said.

"It's just an old rock," said the Snow
Goose.

"That's not a rock," said Posy.

"That's an egg!"

Chapter Three

Posy was right.

It was an egg.

An ENORMOUS egg—as big as a walrus.

It was lumpy. And bumpy. And green.

Dark green with pink spots.

"That is the ugliest egg I have ever seen," said the Snow Goose.

"Ugly egg!" screeched a flock of seagulls.

Posy pressed her head against the lumpy shell. "Don't be mean!" she said. "If there's a chick inside, it will hear you!"

"A good thing, too!" said the Snow
Goose. "We don't want that egg around
here. It's too big and too ugly!"
"Ugly egg! Ugly egg!" screeched the
gulls.
"You should be ashamed of yourselves!"
said Posy.
She flew gently onto the top of the
big green egg.

"This egg is all
alone!" said
Posy. "There
is no one to
keep it warm.
I will sit on it
until it hatches."

The gulls circled high up above Posy
and laughed.

"You're wasting your time with that
ugly old thing," said the Snow Goose.

But Posy took no notice.

For three long, cold weeks, Posy sat on the egg.

WHOOSH! The Arctic wind blew, straight from the North Pole.

It blew so hard that it almost knocked Posy off the egg. But Posy held on tight. She knew that a cold egg will never hatch. Posy had to keep the egg warm. She spread her little wings out as wide as she could. She hugged the lumpy shell. Posy shivered. Puffins normally lay their eggs deep under the ground where it is warm. But the huge spotted egg was much too big to bury in a burrow.

Posy didn't mind. She loved the ugly egg! Even when her orange feet turned blue with cold, she didn't move.

"I wonder what is inside this egg," she said.

It was too big to be a puffin. Or a gull. Or even a snow goose.

CRACK!

"Whatever it is," said the Snow Goose, "that horrible egg is about to hatch!"

Chapter Four

There was a sound like ice breaking.

"Look out!" hissed the Snow Goose.

CRACK!

A big webbed foot slipped out of the

egg.

Out flopped a pair of folded wings.
They were red. And smooth. And
shiny . . .

"There's not a feather on them!" cried
the Snow Goose.

"It's naked!" screeched the gulls.

"Shh!" said Posy. "Don't frighten
him!"

Crack!

Crack!

Out came a long, thick tail.

"Ugly monster!" hissed the Snow
Goose. "It's not a bird at all!"

"It must be a bird," said a seagull. "It
came out of an egg."

The Snow Goose flapped her wings.

"That *thing* is NOT a bird," she said.

"*Eggs*traordinary!" said Mrs. Loon.

"What is it?" screeched the gulls.

25

Posy pushed away the broken eggshell. "Can't you see?" she said. "He's a dragon! A beautiful baby dragon!"

Chapter Five

The dragon staggered to his feet.

"He's so cute!" said Posy.

Flames shot out of the dragon's nose.

"If he's going to breathe fire," said
Mrs. Loon, "you should name him . . .
Burny!"

"Burny?" said Posy. "I like that
name!"

Burny seemed to like that name, too.

SNORT!

FLASH!

He blew out another flame.

"Get that monster away from here,"

hissed the Snow Goose.

"He'll burn our nests with his fiery

breath," cried a gull.

"He'll eat our chicks with his terrible

jaws," warned another.

"Shoo! Shoo!" screeched all the gulls together.

"Don't let Burny burn our nests!" they cried.

The Snow Goose and the gulls flew at the baby dragon. From all across the nest site angry birds came.

"Stop!" cried Posy.

But the birds wouldn't listen.

They flapped their wings. They pecked. They dived. They swooped at the little dragon.

"Shoo, monster! Shoo!" shrieked the gulls.

Birds plunged. Feathers flew!

WHIRL!

SWIRL!

The wind blew up a storm of snow and
feathers.

The birds lunged at Burny again.

They jabbed him with their sharp

claws and beaks.

"Stop!" begged Posy.

But Burny fled.

"Hurrah!" cheered the Snow
Goose. "We've scared the
monster away!"

Chapter Six

Posy flew above the nest site.

"Burny," she called. "Burny, where are you?"

Posy flew out over the deep, cold sea. She flapped high up over the steep gray cliffs and then back over the nest site again.

"Burny's just a baby. He's too young to be alone," she cried.

"And he's too dangerous," said the Snow Goose.

"THERE HE IS!" screeched the gulls. The dragon pup was high up on the rocks. He was crouched beside the Snow Goose's nest.

"He's eating my eggs," shrieked the Snow Goose. "He'll fry them with his breath. He'll gobble them up for breakfast!"

"That's not true," said Posy. "Look! He isn't *eating* your eggs . . . He's keeping them warm!"

In all the fuss, the careless Snow Goose had forgotten to stay in her nest. She had left her eggs alone in the snow. They were getting cold.

WHOOSH! The Arctic wind blew, straight from the North Pole.

But Burny breathed gently.

Puff!

He blew tiny flames of warmth across

the nest.

"My eggs are starting to hatch!" said

the Snow Goose.

The dragon blew gently again.

Puff! Puff!

Seven tiny goslings poked their heads out of the nest.

Posy and Mrs. Loon cheered.

"My babies!" The Snow Goose flew close to the dragon.

"I'm sorry," she said. "I was wrong about you, Burny. You're not a monster. You saved my eggs. You kept them warm."

Burny blew a perfect purple smoke
ring. And he bowed.

"He's so warm-hearted," Mrs. Loon
said with a giggle.
Everyone gathered around the nest.

That night, the Snow Goose was
happy with her seven new goslings.

And Posy had her baby

dragon to care for.

She snuggled under Burny's fiery chin.

WHOOSH! The Arctic wind blew,

straight from the North Pole.

But Posy had never felt so warm in all

her life.

About the author and illustrator

Lou Kuenzler grew up on a sheep farm in Devon, England. She now lives in London with one husband, two children, two cats, and one dog. Lou teaches drama to children and grownups. But, best of all, she likes to write stories. Lou says, "It's a bit like sitting on a big egg and waiting to see what will hatch!"

David Hitch studied illustration at Central Saint Martins College in London, England, where he still lives with his partner. He has been illustrating for more than 15 years. David says, "Just like the dragon hatching the eggs, I like to breathe life into stories with my illustrations."

Strategies for Independent Readers

Predict

Think about the cover, illustrations, and the title
of the book. What do you think this book will be about?
While you are reading think about what may
happen next and why.

Monitor

As you read ask yourself if what you're reading makes sense.
If it doesn't, reread, look at the illustrations, or read ahead.

Question

Ask yourself questions about important ideas
in the story such as what the characters might
do or what you might learn.

Phonics

If there is a word that you do not know, look carefully
at the letters, sounds, and word parts that you do know.
Blend the sounds to read the word. Ask yourself if this is
a word you know. Does it make sense in the sentence?

Summarize

Think about the characters, the setting where the
story takes place, and the problem the characters faced
in the story. Tell the important ideas in the beginning,
middle, and end of the story.

Evaluate

Ask yourself questions like: Did you like the story?
Why or why not? How did the author make the story
come alive? How did the author make the story fun to
read? How well did you understand the story? Maybe
you can understand it better if you read it again!